' "We interrupt this programme to bring you an important newsflash," the announcer said. "Early this morning the Marple Street branch of the First National Savings Bank was raided by a masked gang. The alarm was raised by a passer-by, and police arrived just as the raiders emerged from the bank.

"The gang escaped in a getaway car and a high-speed, cross-country chase ended in the Chandler Street area, where the raiders disappeared . . ."

"Hey!" I said. "That's where my school is!" '

All Sam Marlowe wants is to be a private detective – the very best gumshoe there's ever been. And now it looks as if she's about to get her first big break! A bank robbery case! But why is one of her teachers missing? Sam starts adding two and two together and coming up with a lot more than four . . .

SAM
THE GIRL DETECTIVE
TONY BRADMAN

ILLUSTRATED BY DOFFY WEIR

YEARLING BOOKS

SAM, THE GIRL DETECTIVE
A YEARLING BOOK 0 440 862124

Originally published in Great Britain by Yearling Books

PRINTING HISTORY
Yearling edition published 1989
Reprinted 1991, 1992, 1993

This book is set in 14/16 pt Century Schoolbook
by Colset Private Limited, Singapore.

Yearling Books are published by Transworld Publishers Ltd.,
61–63 Uxbridge Road, Ealing, London W5 5SA,
in Australia by Transworld Publishers (Australia) Pty. Ltd.,
15–25 Helles Avenue, Moorebank, NSW 2170,
and in New Zealand by Transworld Publishers (N.Z.) Ltd.,
3 William Pickering Drive, Albany, Auckland.

Printed and bound in Great Britain by
Cox & Wyman Ltd., Reading, Berks.

SAM, THE GIRL DETECTIVE

Chapter One

I opened a bleary eye and peered at the clock on my bedside cabinet. Mickey Mouse was pointing at the eight with one white-gloved hand, and at the three with the other. I could tell from the smile on Mickey's face that he thought something was pretty funny.

It could only mean one thing – I was going to be late for school. Again.

'Sam! SAMANTHA MARLOWE! Didn't you hear me the first time?' Someone was shouting at me from downstairs. 'Will you *please* get out of that bed? It's quarter past eight!'

'Coming, Mum!' I called back. But

I didn't budge, even though Mickey's hand twitched towards the four. It was lovely and warm under my duvet, and my legs hadn't got round to waking up yet. Perhaps I ought to have let them know it was morning. But there was plenty of time. Maybe even enough for me to read some more of the detective story that had kept most of me awake until late the night before – *Murder at Marvin Mansions*.

I reached out for it, and turned to where I'd folded down the corner of a page. I'd just started Chapter Seven, and already the detective had found two major clues and another corpse. But this morning I couldn't keep my mind on the plot. I was still thinking about what else had happened yesterday evening.

It's tough being a kid. I should know – I've been one all my life. The main problem is having parents. Take mine, for instance (I wish you would). Last night, I'd asked Mum and Dad if I could stay up past my bedtime to watch this terrific detective movie on TV. At first they said OK. But then they'd realized it wouldn't be over until nearly eleven. It didn't matter how much I begged and pleaded, or how loudly I shouted that all my friends are allowed to stay up practically half the night. Dad just stood at the bottom of the stairs doing his Stern Father act, pointing in the direction of my room.

I felt pretty grumpy by the time I'd stamped upstairs to my room, I can tell you. How was I ever going to learn about being a detective with parents like that? They probably want me to be a Miss Goody Two Shoes, the kind of girl who grows up to be a ballet dancer or something totally yucky like a teacher, for heaven's sake. But all I want to be is a private detective, the best gumshoe there's ever been. I want to take on cases and find clues. I want to track down criminals and solve crimes. But what do I get? I get treated like a baby.

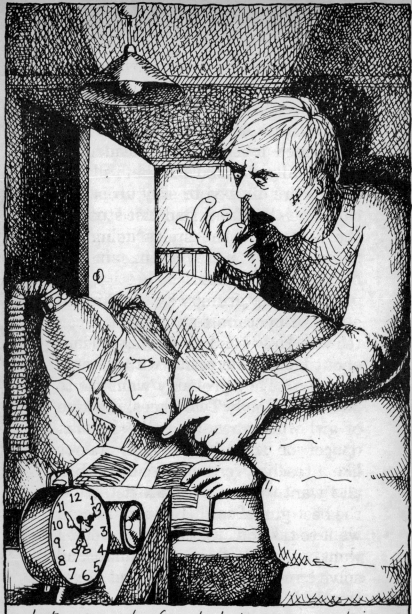

Late enough for dad to come upstairs and perform one of his furious I've-never-seen-anything-like-it tantrums...

So I decided to stay awake late reading, just to get my own back. Late enough for Dad to come upstairs and perform one of his famous I've-never-seen-anything-like-it tantrums. He even gave me one of his you-had-better-pull-your-socks-up lectures, too. When I explained that I don't actually wear any socks in bed, he had gone very red in the face and announced I wouldn't be getting any pocket money for some time. Maybe never. Or even longer.

See what I mean? All that's bad enough. But what makes it a lot worse is that nobody takes me *seriously*.

'Sam! SAM!' There was that voice again. Mum sounded as if she was training to be a foghorn. 'If you're not out of that bed in two seconds, you're going to be in *serious* trouble!'

'I'm out, I'm out,' I shouted back. Mickey's hand was past the four already. I stuck out my tongue at him, threw back the duvet and stood up. My legs were still a little sleepy, but I thought they'd get me to the bathroom. Just.

Once I was there, I looked at myself in the mirror. I pulled the brim of an imaginary hat down over one eye. Sam Marlowe, world-famous girl detective, was ready to face another day. Well, almost.

'Here's looking at you, kid,' I said. And then I started brushing my teeth – very fast . . .

'But Mum, I just can't find it anywhere! And it's got *all* my stuff in it! What am I going to *do*?'

'Ah!' said Dad from behind his newspaper. The radio was playing softly in the background. 'The Case Of The Missing School Bag. So much for the great detective.'

My big brother Philip sniggered. Philip does a lot of sniggering. It's about the only thing he can do well.

'At least my brain isn't missing, stupid,' I said.

'That will do, Sam,' said Dad, putting the newspaper down. Philip just gave me one of his I'll-get-you-back looks.

'I'll give you a clue, Sherlock,' Dad was saying. 'I tripped over something in the hall this morning that felt just like a school bag. If you ask me, it looks like somebody dumped it there after school yesterday and just forgot about it. Why don't you go and investigate?'

I went into the hall. It was all coming back to me now. My bag was in the corner, just as Dad had suspected. I opened it and pulled everything out – pencil case, books, loads of rubbish . . . and my homework, which I suddenly remembered I hadn't done. Again. But the *really* important thing wasn't there.

'If you're looking for that magnifying glass, you left it in the front room,' Mum said. 'I do wish you wouldn't scatter your things around like that, Sam. And shouldn't you be on your way to school by now? It's nearly quarter to nine you know.'

I shot into the front room and grabbed the magnifying glass. I'd borrowed it from my friend Richard to practise looking for clues, and I'd promised faithfully to give it back to him today. It belongs to his dad, who says he needs it for his stamp collection. Richard says he spends more time using it to read the racing results in his paper. Anyway, the problem is that he doesn't know Richard lent it to me, and would probably be a little cross if he found out. Did I say a *little* cross? If he's anything like my dad, he'd probably go totally *hairless*.

I went back into the kitchen to grab a slice of toast to eat on my way to school, and to say goodbye.

'See you later, alligator . . .' I started to say, but just at that moment Philip turned up the sound on the radio.

'Ssh . . . listen!' he said.

'We interrupt this programme to bring you an important newsflash,' the announcer said. 'Early this morning the Marple Street branch of the First National Savings Bank was raided by a masked gang. The alarm was raised by a passer-by, and police arrived just as the raiders emerged from the bank.

'The gang escaped in a getaway car, and a high-speed, cross-town chase ended in the Chandler Street area, where the raiders disappeared . . .'

'Hey!' I said. 'That's where my school is!'

'Ssh!' said Dad.

'It's thought the gang switched cars near Chandler Street School. The police are continuing their inquiries, and are confident of making some arrests soon. We'll bring you reports of any further developments as they happen, so stay tuned. And now, back to the music . . .'

'Wow!' I said. 'The police will probably be all over the street! I'd better get to school before I miss all the excitement . . .'

'Hold on, super-sleuth,' said Dad. 'I've got a few things to say before you rush off . . .'

'Yes, Dad,' I said with a sigh. Here we go, I thought. Another lecture. If there was ever a National Nagging Competition, Dad would win it by a mile. The only problem would be getting him to stop.

'The police will have plenty to do,' he said.

'Yes, Dad.'

'And the last thing they'll want is a nosy kid snooping around trying to play detective. So do you promise you'll stay out of their way?'

'Yes, Dad,' I said. 'I promise.' I put my hands behind my back and crossed my fingers.

This was a chance I couldn't possibly miss . . .

16

Chapter Two

I wish I had a detective's hat. I wish I
had a detective's coat. I wish I had an
office with a door that had my name
on it, and a secretary who took mes-
sages. I wish I knew a friendly cop
who could give me inside information
about crime and criminals.

But most of all I wish I had a fast
car to get me to school, pronto. I need
to be on time at least *once* this week.
It's only the second week of term, and
my teacher, Miss Christie, gave me a
real telling-off yesterday. She's new
at our school, but it hasn't taken us
long to find out she's got a real thing
about being punctual. That's not her

only fault, though. She's got plenty more. She likes giving surprise maths tests, for instance ... but that's another story. A horror story.

'It's the early bird that catches the worm,' she likes to say. Well, Miss Christie arrives early enough to catch every worm in the lawn at the front of the school before they've had a chance to wake up. Some say she gets to school at about eight o'clock, but as no one is ever there before her, it's impossible to tell if it's true. She's certainly been arriving before all the other teachers, even Mr Pinkerton, the headmaster, which gets on his nerves. You can tell by the look on his face when he talks to her.

I know I won't ever be an early bird, mostly because Miss Christie told me so. By the time I get to school, the worms have got up, had breakfast, been shopping and come back, and are thinking about having lunch. So it won't come as any surprise to you that Miss Christie and I aren't getting on as well as we should.

When I hit the corner of Chandler Street, I knew something else, too. I wasn't going to make it. The school playground looked like our kitchen when Dad asks if anyone wants to help him do the washing-up. Everyone was probably inside at their desks, scribbling away. At that very moment, Miss Christie would be standing by the classroom door, looking at her watch, her lips pursed, waiting for me to appear . . .

Then I saw something that made all thoughts of Miss Christie vanish. There before me, right in front of the school gate where they shouldn't be, were several cars. I could tell by the flashing lights and big stripes that two belonged to the police, but the third didn't. A couple of its doors were open, and it was half on the pavement. It was a pretty bad piece of parking. Even my dad could have done better. Eventually.

But the policemen who were standing around weren't worried about the way it was parked. It was robbery that was on their minds. Ah ha, I thought. This must be the getaway car from the Marple Street bank job!

I strolled over, cool and slow, keeping my eyes open for clues. There were skid marks on the street leading to the car, and some more from a spot just in front of it. Those must have been from the car they switched to. The gang had certainly been in something of a hurry to get away. And I don't think it was because they didn't want to buy any tickets to the Annual Police Charity Ball, somehow.

A policeman was kneeling on the pavement beside the car. He had a tin of powder in one hand, and was carefully dusting it on to a door handle with a small brush. I stood close behind him and looked over his shoulder to see how it was done.

'Found any dabs yet?' I said at last. The policeman whirled round, dropped the tin of powder on his blue trousers, and fell backwards into a puddle.

'Now look what you've made me do!' he said. He didn't sound all that pleased to see me. I couldn't think why. 'I'll never get my trousers clean . . . What did you say?'

'Have you found any fingerprints?' I said. I spoke very slowly. Adults, like big brothers, can be pretty thick sometimes. 'They would have worn gloves, though, wouldn't they?'

'And what business of yours is that, Miss?' This new voice came from behind me. Now it was my turn to look round quickly.

When I did, I saw a man in a rain-coat. He was alone, so it was a pretty good bet the voice belonged to him. He was tall, but everything else about him was ordinary, from his ordinary brown shoes to his ordinary, balding head.

'Well, Miss? I'm waiting for an answer,' he said. He sounded just like a teacher. The nasty glare he was giving me was a teacher sort of look, too.

21

Well miss?
I'm waiting for an answer.

The nasty glare he was giving me was a teacher sort of look, too.

'Er ... I don't suppose it's any of my business,' I said. 'I was just interested. I heard about it on the radio this morning. This *is* the get-away car, isn't it?'

'It might be,' said the man. 'And then again, it might not be. That's for me to know, and you to find out. Now why don't you run along like a good little girl and use up some of that curiosity on your school work?' He looked at his watch. 'I'd say you were a little late. And don't just sit there, Constable Dixon. I'd like to see those prints some time this year, if it's all right with you.'

He walked off towards a group of policemen who were examining the skid marks in the road. I felt like sticking my tongue out at him, but I settled instead for wishing someone would make skid marks on his bald head. The only thing I hate more than being called 'miss' by an adult is being told to 'run along like a good little girl'.

'I wouldn't get in his bad books if I were you,' said Constable Dixon. 'That's Inspector Raven of the Yard, one of the best detectives in the world.'

'Oh, is it?' I said. Maybe he wasn't quite so ordinary after all. I stopped thinking nasty thoughts about him. I was beginning to wish I'd woken my legs up a little earlier this morning.

'Has he solved any big cases?' I said. 'Anything that's been on the TV?'

'Oh yes,' said Constable Dixon, with a smile. 'Loads. There was the case of the Rolfe diamonds just last month, and he solved that big murder case last year ...' His smile disappeared. 'Hey, I shouldn't be sitting here talking to you. I've got work to do. Now clear off, will you?'

Just then, Inspector Raven called out.

'Dixon! Will you come over here for a moment, please?'

'Coming, Sir!' said Constable Dixon, saluting. He scuttled over to the group round the skid marks. One of the other policemen gave him the end of a tape measure to hold. He looked as if he could manage that OK. Just.

I ducked down beside the car and pulled the magnifying glass out of my school bag. I ran it over the door handle, and then turned my attention to the back seat. Maybe Inspector Raven would change his tune if I came up with the clue that solved the case . . . But there wasn't much to see. Either Constable Dixon had done a good job, or there were no clues to be had.

I thought it was about time I went into school, anyway. Miss Christie would be furious by now. I could see her in my mind's eye, standing there, tapping her foot in the way she does when she's feeling cross. I stood up and headed for the school gates, feeling pretty sorry for myself.

Then I saw it. Something very interesting, lying underneath the scruffy bush just inside the gates, next to some sweet wrappers and an empty Coke tin.

A lady's shoe. A black one with a small buckle, size five, according to the number on the sole. Not my style, or my size. But the shoe didn't belong to me, so none of that really mattered.

The question was – who *did* it belong to?

I stood there, thinking for a second. Could the shoe have something to do with the bank job? But why would a bank robber be wearing a lady's shoe? I looked over my shoulder at the policemen outside in the street. Maybe it was a clue. And maybe I ought to tell Inspector Raven about my find . . .

But he had told me to run along, hadn't he?

I put the shoe into my bag and dashed across the playground.

Chapter Three

There was a strange feeling about the school that morning. I sensed it as soon as I opened the door and stepped inside. The main corridor was quiet, but there was a simple reason for that. Assembly was over, and everyone was in class, doing lessons. Everyone, that is, who wasn't late like me.

No, it was something else that didn't feel right. And as I walked towards my classroom, it clicked. There was no Miss Christie standing by the door, waiting for me to appear. No Miss Christie staring at me as if I'd just crawled out from underneath a stone. That either meant she'd forgotten about me, which wasn't likely, or I was so late she thought I wasn't coming to school at all.

Either way, I knew I was going to be in big trouble when I opened that door.

But for once in my life I was wrong. Miss Christie wasn't about to tell me off for being late. Neither was she going to give the other kids a hard time for running around and shouting and generally behaving in all the ways grown-ups say they shouldn't. Miss Christie was late herself!

I was so amazed by this news that I had to sit down.

'Tell me I'm dreaming, Richard,' I said. 'I can't believe it.'

'Well, she isn't here, is she?' he said. 'And no one's seen her anywhere in school this morning. So she must be late.'

Richard Watson isn't the cleverest person in the world. In fact, like most boys, he sometimes has problems with really hard things, like remembering to breathe or tying up his shoelaces. But I had to admit he had a point.

Today was getting more interesting by the minute.

'Do you think something's happened to her?' Richard said. I was just about to answer when someone else butted in.

'I don't know why you're asking *her*,' said Steven Greenstreet, my least favourite classmate. '*She* thinks she's a detective, but she can't even find her way to school in the mornings. That's why she's always late.'

Steven was sitting at his desk, a big, stupid grin on his face. He was surrounded by his gang, who were all falling about laughing at his crummy joke. They're mostly pretty ugly, some of them are fat, others are small and nervous. I won't bother telling you their names. Let's just call them Grumpy (that's Steven), Bumpy, Lumpy, Stumpy and Jumpy, otherwise known as The Feeble Five.

They're very, very boring. So boring, just looking at them makes me feel sleepy. But as you can probably tell, they think they're hilarious. And their favourite game is hanging around making fun of *me*.

'Why don't you go play with the traffic, Greenstreet?' I said, looking at my nails, as cool as could be. 'On second thoughts, you'd better stay in school. If anyone spots you outside, they'll think we've been invaded by monsters from space and start a panic.'

'Ha, ha, very funny ... I don't think,' said Steven. 'And anyway, Little Miss Detective, shouldn't you be outside helping the police? Or didn't you notice they were there when you arrived?'

'Everyone thinks that's the getaway car from the bank raid that was on the news this morning,' said one of The Feeble Five. I think it might have been Stumpy, but I can't be sure. I try not to look at them too closely if I can help it.

'Yeah,' said another one. It could have been Lumpy. 'Old Pinkerton made us all come in early. He said we weren't to stand around staring at the police.' That sounded just like Mr Pinkerton. His hobby is thinking up as many ways as he can of stopping kids from having any fun.

'I saw them, all right,' I said, giving him one of my cool, grown-up smiles. 'I had a talk with one of the detectives, actually. His name's Inspector Raven.'

'Cor!' said Richard. 'Hasn't he been on TV? What did he say?'

I could see The Feeble Five were pretty impressed, even though they were trying their hardest not to show it.

'Oh, he just asked me if I'd seen anything suspicious,' I said. 'I gave him a couple of clues, then I came into school.'

'Wow!' said Richard.

'I don't believe it,' said Steven with

a sneer. 'She's making it up. She's just a stupid girl who doesn't know anything.'

'That's what you think,' I said. 'But then you've got no idea what I found down by the big dustbins behind the kitchens, have you?'

The nasty sneer disappeared from Steven's face. That was because his jaw dropped, and not even an idiot like Grumpy can sneer with his mouth open.

'What *did* you find?' he said. He couldn't hide the fact that he was really interested.

'That's for me to know, and you to find out,' I said. 'Why don't you run along like a good little boy at morning play and investigate?'

Now you know, and I know, that I hadn't been anywhere near the dustbins. But I needed to make sure The Feeble Five didn't follow me around later on. I had some investigating of my own to do, and giving them a false lead would get them off my back.

Besides, with any luck, Greenstreet and his gang would fall into a dustbin and get taken away to the city dump. And that would make me very happy.

'I might do that,' said Steven, 'I might just do that . . .'

He said a lot more, but I wasn't listening. I'd noticed something very odd in the corner of the classroom, just behind his desk.

The doors to Miss Christie's stationery cupboard were shut, which wasn't unusual. But there was a big metal chain looped round the door handles, with a shiny brass padlock attached to it. And that *was* unusual.

Miss Christie is very proud of her stationery cupboard. She took an interest in it from the moment she started at the school. It's bigger than it looks from the outside, but she keeps it amazingly tidy. She knows exactly where everything is, and how much paper or how many exercise books she's got.

She usually keeps it locked, but the

padlock and chain were new. I stood up and casually walked to the back of the classroom to have a closer look. That's when I noticed the faint marks on the floor leading to the cupboard doors. It was odd, but they reminded me of something I'd seen before. I just couldn't think what it was, though . . .

What did it all mean? I was beginning to put a few thoughts together when the classroom door flew open and Mr Pinkerton strode in.

'Right, you lot!' he shouted. 'Settle down, will you. As you *may* have noticed, Miss Christie isn't with us this morning . . .'

'What's wrong with her, Sir?' said Richard.

'I'm afraid you know as much as I do, Ronald,' said Mr Pinkerton, crossly. He never gets anyone's name right. 'We don't seem to be able to contact her.'

'Does that mean you're going to send us home, Sir?' said Steven.

'That's what you did when it snowed last year and the heating broke down.'

'I'm sorry, Simon,' said Mr Pinkerton, 'but no such luck. I'm going to be looking after you myself today. Everyone else is busy and I haven't got time to find a replacement.'

We all groaned. Miss Christie is a pretty strict teacher who makes us work hard, but if anything, Mr Pinkerton is even more of a slave driver.

'I think we'll start with a maths test,' he said. We groaned some more. 'Get out your exercise books. How good are you at multiplying fractions?'

Just then, the door opened and a man walked in.

'Can I help you?' said Mr Pinkerton. He looked rather surprised.

'Er ... yeah,' said the man. 'I'm a teacher. I'm here to stand in for Miss Christie ...'

Chapter Four

He said his name was Mr Clyde, and I'd never seen a teacher like him before. He was big, for starters – very big. Mr Pinkerton's no shorty, but next to Mr Clyde he looked like a friend of Snow White's. Correction – he looked like one of The Seven Dwarfs' little brothers.

It wasn't just Mr Clyde's size that made us all stare at him with our mouths open, though. He didn't dress much like any teacher we'd ever had, either. He was wearing a grey jacket that was so shiny you could have used it for a mirror. He didn't have a tie on, probably because he'd never be able

to find one to match his shirt, which
had bright green and yellow stripes.
Just looking at it gave me a headache.

I decided to concentrate on his face
instead. It was the sort of face you
usually see on boxers. He had a few
scars, but it was his nose that was
really interesting. He stood facing
Mr Pinkerton, but most of his nose

was pointing in a completely different direction.

'I'm afraid I don't understand, Mr Clark,' said Mr Pinkerton at last. 'I haven't done anything about getting a replacement for Miss Christie, so how did you know we needed someone?'

'Miss Christie told me herself. We're old friends,' said Mr Clyde with a big smile. His teeth were even more dazzling than his jacket. 'She's not too well, you see, and when she knew she wouldn't be coming in today, she asked me to fill in for her. She thought it would save you a lot of bother.'

Mr Pinkerton's eyebrows moved towards each other like hairy caterpillars who want a cuddle. It's always a sure sign that he's cross.

'Well, really, Mr Clark, this is most irregular,' he said. '*Most* irregular. It's not Miss Christie's responsibility to do that sort of thing. And why hasn't she rung me herself?'

'Er . . . she didn't get much sleep

last night,' said Mr Clyde, 'so she's gone back to bed. She'll probably want to talk to you a little later.'

'It just isn't good enough, I'm afraid.' Mr Pinkerton said. We were all sitting on the edge of our seats, as quiet as could be. This was much more fun than having a maths test. And of course, once Mr Pinkerton realized that, he soon decided to put a stop to our enjoyment.

'I think we'd better talk about this outside, Mr Clark,' he said, looking round at the class. 'Right, you lot, it's time you got on with some work.'

Mr Pinkerton found a page of long division problems in our maths book and told us to do as many as we could. Then he went into the corridor, followed by Mr Clyde, who had to duck. Mr Clyde gave us a big wink before he closed the door behind him.

There was silence for a second, and then we all scrambled for the door. I was just in front of Steven, and we had a brief tussle over the handle. I won, and eased the door open slightly. It felt as if the entire class was breathing down my neck.

'Can you hear what they're saying?' said Steven.

'Not when you're shouting in my ear like that,' I hissed at him. 'Just try and keep that big mouth of yours buttoned up, will you?'

Luckily, the two of them hadn't gone very far. Lucky for me because they were both speaking very softly, and I really had to strain to catch their voices.

'You'll have to tell me more about yourself, Mr Clark,' Mr Pinkerton was saying. He still sounded cross. 'For instance, where was your last job?'

'Oh, I've done jobs all over the place,' said Mr Clyde. He gave Mr Pinkerton another of those dazzling smiles.

'And where did you do your training?'

'I did a spell at er . . . Wandsworth,'

said Mr Clyde. 'And a couple of stretches at Pentonville. That's where I really learnt a lot.'

'I didn't know there was a teacher's training college in that area,' said Mr Pinkerton. He was frowning so much now that the two hairy caterpillars on his forehead had completely joined together. He was about to ask another question, but Mr Clyde got in first.

'They look quite a handful, that class,' he said.

'They are,' said Mr Pinkerton. 'Class Nine is the worst class in the school. I wasn't looking forward to teaching them myself today, I can tell you . . .'

'What a cheek!' said Steven in my ear.

'Sssh!' I said. 'I can't hear what they're saying!'

'I think I could manage them,' said Mr Clyde. 'I specialize in . . . er, handling troublemakers.'

'Oh, really?' said Mr Pinkerton. Suddenly he looked a lot more cheerful.

There were now two hairy caterpillars on his forehead again, both of them doing little dances. 'Why didn't you tell me before? That sounds just what Class Nine needs. Carry on, Mr Clark. Glad to have you aboard. I'll need to have your references and do the paperwork, of course . . .'

He held out his hand, and Mr Clyde shook it. Mr Pinkerton winced, and the hairy caterpillars shot back towards each other. He seemed to be in some pain.

'Can't we sort all that out later?' said Mr Clyde. 'I'd better get stuck into Class Nine before they start causing trouble, don't you think?' Mr Pinkerton just nodded, looked down at his mangled fingers, then walked along the corridor to his office.

Mr Clyde turned sharply on his heel and headed back towards us. He was chuckling quietly and shaking his head. For some reason he seemed to be very pleased with himself.

'Quick, everyone!' I said. 'Back to

your seats! He's coming!'

By the time Mr Clyde opened the classroom door, we were all back in our seats, heads down over our books, quietly pretending to work our way through those long division problems.

Mr Clyde walked up to Miss Christie's desk and sat on her chair. He leaned back and put his feet on the desk. As they were pretty big, they didn't leave room for much else.

'Well, well,' he said, showing us those gleaming teeth again. They reminded me of something, and at first I couldn't think what it was. Then a picture flashed into my mind. Not a very nice picture, either. I'd seen a film about a shark once. Sharks have got lots of teeth, too. Sharp, white teeth.

'Well, well,' he said again. 'Isn't this cosy. Who'd have thought I'd ever end up doing this?'

'Doing what, Sir?' said Steven, brightly. He's always been the sort of creep who plays up to teachers.

'Never you mind, sonny,' said Mr Clyde, picking up a ruler that was on the desk in front of him. He stopped smiling, swung his feet off the desk, and gave Steven a look which would have withered one of my mum's pot plants instantly. It certainly made Steven look pretty wilted.

'I think we'd better get a few things straight,' said Mr Clyde. He stood up and walked towards the back of the class. 'Let's start as we mean to go on. I'm the sort of teacher who likes a bit of quiet. We'll get along fine so long as you keep yourselves busy and don't bother me. But if there's any trouble . . .'

He stopped by Steven's desk. He held the ruler out in front of him in both hands, and snapped it in two with a loud crack. Steven looked up and gulped.

'Do we understand each other now, Class Nine?'

'Yes, Sir!' everyone squeaked.

'That's fine, Class Nine,' said Mr

Clyde. There were those dazzling teeth again. He walked behind Steven and came to the stationery cupboard. He bent down and looked closely at the shining brass padlock I'd noticed. He reached out and shook it gently.

He reached out and shook it gently

'Er, what shall we do to keep ourselves busy, Sir?' said Steven. Mr Clyde straightened up and looked at him.

'What were you all doing when I came in just now?' he said.

'Some maths problems, Sir,' said Steven.

'I think I can come up with a few more of those for you,' said Mr Clyde. 'OK – write this down. If it takes one bank robber two hours to count a haul of fifty thousand pounds, how long would it take *three* villains to count it? That's supposing they don't start arguing, of course, or slipping money in their back pockets. Now who knows the answer? No cheating, mind.'

Like I say – today was becoming more interesting by the second . . .

Chapter Five

The maths problems Mr Clyde set us were different, to say the least. Most of them seemed to be about bank robbers, although there was one involving a jail. Mr Clyde drew a map of a prison on the blackboard, complete with the positions of the warders and when they changed their shifts. We had to work out the best escape route on pieces of paper. Mr Clyde collected them all in, but he didn't mark them. He just slipped them in his pocket.

I couldn't keep my mind on maths, though. I was doing some working out of a different kind. I was adding two and two and coming up with a lot more than four, which wouldn't have surprised Miss Christie. But I was beginning to wonder whether she might have a few problems of her own. Problems you couldn't solve on a blackboard or in an exercise book.

'There's something very strange going on in this school,' I said to Richard at morning play. We were standing in the corner of the playground, as far away from the school buildings and all the other kids as we could get. I wanted some peace and quiet while I thought a few things through.

'My mum says there's a tummy bug going round,' said Richard. 'That's probably what Miss Christie's got. There's three away in our class, and I know for a fact that Josie's got it.'

Sometimes Richard amazes me. I always think he can't possibly say anything more stupid than some of the things he's come out with in the

49

past. And then he goes ahead and does exactly that.

'That's not what I had in mind, Richard,' I said with a sigh. He looked confused. 'Don't you think it's a bit of a coincidence that Miss Christie should be ill on the day robbers leave their getaway car outside our school?'

'I don't see what you're getting at,' he said, scratching his head.

'It just seems funny to me that Miss Christie hasn't rung the school,' I said. 'And she's not answering her phone, either.' On our way out to the playground we'd walked past Mr Pinkerton's office, and I'd heard him telling the school secretary to keep ringing Miss Christie till she got through.

'She's the sort of teacher who likes everyone to follow the rules – that includes herself. I reckon she'd have to be in a really bad way before she did something like that. Unless someone's stopping her from talking to anyone on the phone.'

Richard looked even more confused now.

'I still don't see what you're getting at,' he said.

'What I'm getting at, brainbox, is that I think Miss Christie might have been . . . kidnapped!'

Richard's mouth fell open.

'Cor!' he said. 'Who do you think would do a thing like that?'

'The bank robbers, you dummy!' I said.

'But why would they kidnap *our* teacher? What's she got to do with a bank robbery?'

'Nothing. But I reckon she arrived at school at the same time as the robbers did. She probably saw them jumping out of one getaway car and getting into another. That means she'd be able to identify them. So they kidnapped her to stop her from helping the police. I'll bet they're holding her somewhere right now. They won't let her go until the heat dies down.'

'What heat?' said Richard.

I tried hard to keep my patience. It was pretty tough. I pointed towards the school gate. The getaway car was still there, and so were the police cars. 'I mean the police, mastermind. They'll be combing everywhere for the robbers. So they'll have to lie low for now.'

I didn't go into any more detail. For some reason I didn't think the time was right to mention the shoe I'd found, even though I was now sure it usually spent most of its time on Miss Christie's foot. Nor did I mention my other suspicions, the ones about the stationery cupboard and our interesting replacement teacher, Mr Clyde.

'Shouldn't we tell someone?' asked Richard. 'Someone like the police, or Mr Pinkerton?'

'They'd never believe us,' I said. 'We're just kids to them. They wouldn't even listen. No, we've got to find some proof before we even try to tell them. And I've got a pretty good idea where I might get it.'

Richard looked as if he had a few more questions to ask, but he didn't get around to them. Instead, he started to sniff.

'What's that awful smell?' he said. I wanted to know the answer to that one myself. I didn't have to wait too long, either.

I looked over Richard's shoulder and saw The Feeble Five approaching. They looked even worse than usual, and the closer they got, the stronger the awful smell became.

'You'd better tell us what you found in the dustbins, or else,' said Steven. 'We searched in them for ages, but we didn't find a thing.'

'Oh, I don't know,' I said. 'You seem to have found plenty of rubbish. Isn't that some cabbage from yesterday's school dinners in your hair?'

'I suppose you think sending us on a wild goose chase was very funny,' said Steven. He looked more like he'd been on a wild cabbage chase. 'You never found anything there in the first place, did you?'

'Maybe I did, and maybe I didn't,' I said. 'And I never said anything about looking *in* the dustbins, did I, Richard?'

'No, you didn't,' said Richard. He could hardly stop himself from giggling. Steven was on the verge of saying something else, but I didn't give him a chance.

'I'll tell you something, Green-street,' I said. 'I found something *much* more interesting down by the school gate. I was just going over to investigate a little more . . .'

'Don't try and kid me,' he said. 'It's another bluff, and I'm not falling for it this time.'

'That's fine by me,' I said. 'I wouldn't want you stamping your great big feet all over any clues that might be there.'

Steven suddenly seemed to be having a lot of problems controlling his face. He didn't want me to think he was fooled. But at the same time, he didn't know whether I might be telling the truth. And if I wasn't telling the truth, what *did* I know? Poor Steven. I almost felt sorry for him. He looked as if his brain was over-heating.

'Come on, lads,' he said at last. 'We don't need a stupid girl to help us. We can find our own clues.'

The Feeble Five ran off across the playground, leaving behind them a trail of cabbage leaves and other things too nasty to mention. I knew exactly where they'd be heading as soon as they thought I wasn't looking. Sometimes I wish they were a little harder to fool. It would make life more of a challenge, anyway.

'I'll bet they go straight off to the gate,' said Richard.

'Of course they will, Richard,' I said.

'But suppose they find something?'

'They couldn't find a bar of chocolate in a sweet-shop,' I said. 'Anyway, don't worry about them – we've got something much more important to do.'

I led Richard back towards the school. We came to the side door nearest our classroom. No one was around, so I slipped in, dragging Richard behind me.

'But you know we're not allowed in during play time!' he whispered to me as we stood in the corridor. 'Suppose somebody sees us!'

'Stop whining,' I said. 'The teachers are all in the staffroom drinking tea and killing themselves with cigarettes. You keep watch by the door while I go in and check up on a few things.'

'But Sam . . .' Richard started to say. I took no notice. I opened the classroom door and peeked round it, just to make sure our friend Mr Clyde wasn't still in there.

He wasn't. I eased in and closed the door behind me. I went over to my desk and pulled the magnifying glass out of my bag. Then I went to the back of the class. It was the stationery cupboard I was interested in – and those marks on the floor.

I couldn't tell much from the padlock and chain, other than that they'd be pretty hard to get off if you didn't have the key. There weren't any scratches or anything else unusual on the cupboard doors, either.

I knelt down to examine the marks

on the floor. If only I could remember what they reminded me of . . . Then it came to me. They were just like the wavy line Dad had made in the back garden the other day when he'd dragged a sack full of grass and leaves to the incinerator.

I didn't have much time to mull this over. The door banged open, and Mr Clyde came marching in.

'Well, well,' he said with a big smile. It made me think of a shark again. A shark who's about to have his dinner. 'What have we here?'

Chapter Six

If you're wondering why Richard hadn't warned me, the answer is simple. I soon noticed that Mr Clyde was holding him by one of his ears. Richard didn't look at all happy about this situation. I think that had something to do with him having a hard time keeping his feet on the floor.

'Don't tell me,' said Mr Clyde, advancing down the classroom in my direction. Richard's face had gone a funny colour, and he was making strange noises. 'Let me guess. Your dad's a policeman, and you do this sort of thing as a hobby.'

'No, Sir,' I said. 'It's all part of my

science project. I'm studying insects.' I slipped the magnifying glass into the pocket of my skirt, and pointed at the floor. There was, in fact, a spider beside Steven's desk. It was lying on its back and didn't look too well. But then neither would you if some smelly giant had picked you up and pulled all your legs off one by one. I just hoped something similar wasn't going to happen to me.

'Oh yeah?' said Mr Clyde. He gave me one of those plant-withering stares and came a little closer.

'Ah, you're in here then, Mr Clark.' Mr Pinkerton was standing at the door. I'd never been so glad to see him. 'Young Watkins there giving you a spot of trouble?'

'Er . . . not really,' said Mr Clyde, letting go of Richard's ear. It stayed bent and glowed very red. 'I don't think he'll give me any bother in future, either.' He ruffled Richard's hair and gave Mr Pinkerton one of his dazzling smiles.

'Jolly good,' said Mr Pinkerton. 'I'm glad to see you getting to grips with things. Anyway, I just popped in to say there's a special assembly this morning. I want the whole school in the hall at eleven o'clock sharp.'

'What's all that in aid of then?' said Mr Clyde.

'It's a bit of a nuisance, really,' said Mr Pinkerton. 'The police have asked if they can talk to the school about that bank robbery and the getaway car. I can't see why myself, but the officer in charge was very insistent. And I do believe that we should co-operate with the police. It sets the children a good example, don't you think?'

Mr Clyde had gone quite pale.

'You mean the cops . . . I mean, the police are coming *here*?' he said.

'That's right, Mr Clark,' said Mr Pinkerton. 'I'll see you in the hall with Class Nine at eleven. We'll put them at the back. They shouldn't be able to do too much mischief there, although you never know with Class Nine . . .'

Mr Pinkerton walked out of the door, but came straight back again.

'I've just remembered, Mr Clark, there *was* something else I wanted to talk to you about.'

He came over to Mr Clyde and started whispering to him. But I leaned forward and could just hear what he was saying.

'I've been informed that you were playing cards in the staffroom with several of the other teachers. Someone said it was poker, and that the stakes were quite high. Now I'm not sure this is altogether a good idea. Could we discuss it in my office? I'll see you there in five minutes.'

Mr Pinkerton went out, and stayed out this time. Mr Clyde stood looking at the door for a moment. His fists were clenched, although he wasn't quite so pale any more. I could almost hear the wheels going round inside his head.

He didn't have time to say or do

anything, though. The bell rang for the end of morning play, and everyone started pouring back into the classroom. The Feeble Five were the last ones in. They brought their own special smell with them.

'Right, boys and girls,' said Mr Clyde when we were sitting at our desks. 'I think you've got plenty to keep you busy. I've just got to pop out for a moment.'

He went to the door. He turned to look at me once more just before he made his exit. He didn't say anything. He didn't have to.

His eyes said it all for him.

A little later I was standing in line, waiting to go into the hall with the rest of the class for the special assembly. There was the usual chaos. Teachers were shouting, infants were howling, big children were pushing and shoving. But I wasn't taking any notice. I had too much to think about.

A picture was beginning to form in

my mind. A picture of robbers with a heavy sack full of money who were spotted by Miss Christie as she arrived at school early in the morning. What if they'd grabbed her, and in the struggle she'd lost her shoe? That would mean a delay in switching to the second getaway car. The police must have been pretty close behind them.

And what do robbers do sometimes when they're being chased? They hide the loot, split up, and come back for it later. Suppose that's what these robbers had done? And where could they hide a big sack full of stolen money? The stationery cupboard seemed as good a place as any.

All I needed now was proof that some of the robbers had actually come into the school. If I could only get a peek into the cupboard . . . I wondered where they'd got the chain and pad-lock, and who had the key. Whoever it was might have the answer to the whole mystery.

'You haven't seen Mr Clark, have you, Sally?' It was Mr Pinkerton. He meant Mr Clyde. 'I asked him to come to my office, but he hasn't turned up.'

'No, Sir,' I said. 'I haven't seen him since the end of morning play.'

'How irritating,' said Mr Pinkerton. He went into the hall, muttering under his breath about how difficult it was to get good staff these days. We filed in behind him.

I wasn't at all surprised that Mr Clyde had gone missing. I had a pretty good idea now where he fitted into the picture.

He was no teacher. He was one of the robbers.

He'd come back either to get the money from the stationery cupboard, or to make sure that nobody interfered with it. And if he was a robber, he was probably known to the police – which was why he'd gone pale when Mr Pinkerton had told him about the special assembly. He wasn't going to let himself be spotted by a detective as brilliant as Inspector Raven.

It had been Mrs Thomas, Class Eight's teacher, who had told us to go down to the hall at eleven o'clock. She'd come in to see why we were making so much noise. Correction – why everyone else, and especially Steven and the rest of The Feeble Five, had been making so much noise. I'd been too busy thinking things over.

'Quiet please, everybody.' Mr Pinkerton was standing on the stage, looking down at the whole school. His deputy, Mrs Patel, was sitting just behind him, next to Inspector Raven and Constable Dixon. 'I've brought you all together this morning because Inspector Craven has got something very important to say.'

Inspector Raven stood up and walked to one side of the stage, where a large, portable blackboard had been set up. Someone had chalked a rough map of the school on it. The Inspector was just about to start speaking, when Mr Pinkerton decided he hadn't finished.

'What *is* that awful smell?' he said. 'It seems to be coming from the back of the hall. Could you open a few windows please, Mrs Thomas? I'll have to have a word with the cleaners . . .'

The whole school turned to look at Class Nine. Each of The Feeble Five looked embarrassed, although it was hard to tell if they were actually blushing or not. They were still pretty grubby.

'Right, Inspector,' said Mr Pinkerton. 'Over to you.'

'Thank you, Headmaster,' said Inspector Raven. 'Good morning, children.'

'Good morning, Inspector,' we all said.

'You probably know there was a big robbery at a bank near here this morning. We now have pretty good evidence that suggests some of the robbers may actually have come into your school . . .'

Ah ha, I thought. I was right!

'We also have reason to believe that one of you may be in possession of a vital clue that could help us catch these dangerous villains.'

I looked round the hall. There was only one person that could apply to.

And that person was . . . me!

Chapter Seven

It sounded as though Inspector
Raven knew something about a
certain shoe that was sitting in my
school bag. If he did, I was in big
trouble. I could almost feel the hand-
cuffs snapping round my wrists. In
my mind I could see my mum crying
as Constable Dixon led me off to jail.

But I wasn't about to start a
criminal record. Not yet, anyway.
Inspector Raven hadn't finished
talking.

'We know the robbers came into the
school grounds because we found
this,' he said. He held up a black
object. It looked a bit like a balaclava,

one of those woolly winter hats that cover your entire head except for your face. But this only had eye holes, which meant it would make a pretty good mask if you were thinking of robbing a bank.

And that's just what it had been used for, explained the Inspector. He said it had been found by the side entrance to the school, the one on Hammett Avenue, pointing to it on the blackboard as he talked.

'Now we know there were four robbers because they were seen leaving the bank,' he said. 'So it seems reasonable to suppose they split up. Some of them probably got away in a second car that was parked in Chandler Street. We think at least one must have come into the playground, and run round the school building to the Hammett Avenue gate, where he took off his mask and dropped it.

'There may have been another car waiting there. This robber may have escaped on foot. But whatever they all did, we think they may well have left some more clues. And that's where *you* can help.'

He went on to say that if anyone had found something that shouldn't be in the school, or come across anything unusual, like a broken window or a damaged lock, they were to tell a teacher immediately.

'And one last thing,' he said. 'We suspect this robbery was the work of the gang led by a criminal mastermind known only as The Shadow. Very little is known about this villain, except that he's an expert at disguise and meticulous planning. But there's a special reward for his capture, so keep your eyes peeled!'

Inspector Raven sat down, and Mr Pinkerton stood up again. He rambled on like he usually does in assembly, and for a second I thought he was going to tell us to start singing a hymn. But he pulled himself together, said thank you to the Inspector, and also that he was sure we'd all try our best to be very helpful.

Inspector Raven had certainly been helpful to me. He'd given me some information I didn't have. Thanks to him, my picture of what had happened this morning was now a lot fuller. In fact, I had a strong suspicion I knew a lot more about this case than he did.

He obviously had no idea the robbers had actually come into the school *building*. He thought they'd stayed in the playground and gone *round* it. I knew different. Or at least, I thought I did. I didn't have any proof yet. And I didn't have much time left, either. I couldn't keep quiet about what I knew for very much longer. But would Inspector Raven believe me?

That was a risk I'd have to take. I wished I could tie the whole caper up in a pretty little parcel with a bow on top, and hand it to him. But I couldn't. I was going to have to talk to him anyway, and lay out everything I knew. I just hoped he'd buy my story, even without proof. If he didn't, things looked bad for me – and a lot worse for Miss Christie. She was obviously in the hands of The Shadow, who sounded like a very interesting criminal. Someone only a genius of a detective could pin down.

A genius like Sam Marlowe, maybe.

Mr Pinkerton announced that the special assembly was over. The hall started to empty in the usual way, with more shouting from the teachers, more infants howling, and more pushing and shoving from the big kids. I noticed that no one was pushing or shoving The Feeble Five, though. Everyone was giving them as much room as you would an elephant with bad breath. And that's about what they smelt like. Or maybe a little worse.

'Psst!' At first I thought it was a tyre running over a nail. Then I realized it was Richard. 'Psst! Sam!' He was signalling to me. I went over to him. We slipped out of the stream of kids flowing out of the hall. We stood behind a big model of a robot Class Four had made out of old toilet roll tubes and silver paper.

'Well?' I whispered. 'Spill it.' I thought I had a pretty good idea what he wanted to say. He was going to tell me I had to talk to Inspector Raven.

But I was wrong for the second time that day.

'It's Mr Clyde, Sam,' he said, rubbing his ear, the one Mr Clyde had taken such a liking to. 'He's been acting in a very strange way.'

'So what's new?' I said. 'He's the strangest teacher I've ever known, and I've met quite a few. And keep your voice down, will you?'

'But he's been doing something *really* odd,' said Richard. He looked over his shoulder, then leant closer. 'I think he's been hiding.'

'What do you mean, hiding?'

Richard took a deep breath, then told me his story. One of Richard's problems is that he's always going to the toilet. He just can't hold it in for

Richard took a deep breath, then told me his story

longer than five minutes. It drives Miss Christie mad, although at that moment I thought she would have been quite happy to see him hopping up and down asking to be excused.

So Richard had gone to the boys' toilets just before the special assembly. They're at the Hammett

Avenue end of the school, in a little block of their own that's separate from the main building. Next door to them is a hut where we keep a lot of big equipment that won't fit in anywhere else. The PTA uses it to store things in, too.

Just as Richard was coming out of the boys' toilet, he'd seen someone slipping into the hut. Someone wearing a shiny jacket and the sort of shirt that gave you a headache if you looked at it too long. And that someone was Mr Clyde . . .

'So that's where he is!' I said.

'He was acting very suspiciously, too,' said Richard. 'He kept looking over his shoulder, as if he was making sure no one was around. I ducked back into the toilet, so I don't think he saw me.'

My mind started racing. Mr Clyde wanted to keep out of Inspector Raven's way, for sure. But maybe he had another reason for visiting the hut at the Hammett Avenue end of school. This morning's visitors had left a mask behind, hadn't they? So maybe they'd left something else behind, too. Something you might come across if you cared to look in the hut.

Some proof that might tie Mr Clyde to the robbery and Miss Christie's disappearance.

There was no time to lose.

'Thanks, Richard,' I said. I heard him call my name, but I took no notice. I raced down the corridor through the crowds of kids heading back to their classrooms. I came to the double doors at the end, and pushed them open.

The boys' toilets were just in front of me. The hut was to my left. Its door was shut tight. No one was around.

I crept quickly and quietly over to the hut. I put an ear to the door, but all I could hear was my heart thudding. I knew there was a small window in the side facing away from the school. The only way I'd find out if Mr

Clyde was still in there was to slide round and try and get a peek through that window.

So that's what I did. I held my breath as I sneaked around with my back to the hut's wooden walls. I knelt down below the window, let my breath out and tried to stay calm. Then I stood up slowly, and carefully looked over the windowsill.

My luck was in. Not only was Mr Clyde still in the hut, but he had a couple of friends with him too. And one of them, whose face I couldn't see, was just handing Mr Clyde a key. The sort of key that might open a shiny, brass padlock.

That was all the proof I needed.

But then my luck ran out, for just as I was about to turn and run back to the school, I felt a hand over my mouth.

Then everything went black.

Chapter Eight

If you're thinking everything had gone black because there'd been a sudden total eclipse of the sun, then you're wrong. Whoever the hand belonged to had simply put a bag over my head and bundled me into the hut.

I heard the door being shut, and a lot of whispering. I couldn't move, however much I tried. Strong hands held me from behind. I made up my mind to scream as loudly as I could and hope that someone heard me. I opened my mouth – but that's as far as I got.

The bag was pulled off my head, and I found myself staring straight at

Mr Clyde. He gave me one of his dazzling smiles, and I tried very hard not to think about sharks.

'I wouldn't do that if I were you,' he said. I shut my mouth.

'If you were me you'd be standing here with your arms behind your back,' I said. 'And if I were you, I'd let you go before I really got into trouble.'

'Did you hear that, Ron?' said Mr Clyde to the man standing beside him. He was even bigger and more mean-looking than Mr Clyde. 'I told you she was a smart kid.'

'Looks like she's too smart for her own good,' said Ron.

'You might be right there,' said Mr Clyde. 'Are you sure there was no one else with her, Bernie?'

'*Dead* sure,' said a voice that came from behind me and about a metre or two above my head. I twisted round to have a peek at the third man. He was even bigger than Ron, and looked as if he ate children for breakfast.

There was no doubt about it. I was

in something of a tight spot.

'You'll never get away with it,' I said. I tried to keep my voice as calm as possible. I wasn't going to let them see I was scared, even if I was.

'Get away with what, exactly, young lady?' said Mr Clyde.

'The Marple Street bank robbery, of course,' I said.

'I knew this job wouldn't go right,' I heard Ron mutter. 'My horoscope in the paper said I'd be better off staying at home today . . .'

'Shut up, you idiot!' hissed Mr Clyde out of the side of his mouth. He looked at me and turned on his dazzling smile again. 'And what makes you think I'd have anything to do with a bank robbery? I'm just a teacher, aren't I? You know that, er . . . I'm sorry, I never did catch your name.'

'That's because I didn't throw it at you,' I said. I looked him straight in the eye. 'It's Marlowe, Sam Marlowe. That happens to be my *real* name,

Mr Clyde. What's yours?'

The dazzling smile disappeared. It was just as if it had been turned off with a switch.

'OK, kid,' said Mr Clyde. 'Let's both stop playing around. You'd better tell us what you know – and fast. Talk.'

I didn't say a word. But then something happened that meant I didn't have to for a while.

'Quiet, everybody!' whispered Ron suddenly. 'I think I can hear someone coming!'

'Get down!' said Mr Clyde. 'And if she so much as squeaks, Bernie, you know what to do.' Strange man, Mr Clyde. One minute he wanted me to talk, the next he didn't. Bernie pulled me down and held a hand over my mouth.

There were footsteps and loud voices outside the hut. It was probably some boys heading for the toilets. I don't know why it is, but boys can never do anything without making as much noise as possible.

'Who is it?' Ron whispered.

'I don't know, do I?' hissed Mr
Clyde. He sounded as bad-tempered
as a snake that someone's tied in a
knot. They hissed and whispered at
each other a lot more. It made me
think of a couple of cobras having a
spitting contest.

'I think they've gone,' said Ron at last. Bernie lifted me to my feet. I was being stared at by Mr Clyde again.

'So what are we going to do with her?' said Bernie.

'Whatever we do, we'd better do it fast,' said Ron. 'Even if she hasn't told anybody, someone might start looking for her. Don't they have a register or something? I don't want to be around when they find her.'

'Don't panic,' said Mr Clyde. 'If you'd seen Class Nine you'd realize they might *want* to lose one or two of them for a while. She won't be missed for ages.'

'You can't be sure of that,' said Ron. 'And we can't hang around here all day. Suppose someone wants something out of this hut?'

Mr Clyde glanced nervously towards the door, then turned back to me. He chewed a fingernail for a while. He looked as if he was having trouble making his mind up about something.

'There's nothing for it,' he said at

last. 'We'll have to take her to . . .'

'You don't mean. . .' said Ron. Even in the darkness of the hut I could see he'd gone pale.

'I do, Ron, I do,' said Mr Clyde. 'We'll have to take her to . . . The Shadow!'

I didn't have a chance to say anything. Ron opened the door and peered out to see if the coast was clear. Then Bernie picked me up, slung me under one arm and left the hut at a run. Mr Clyde followed close behind.

By the time Bernie had jogged a couple of metres he'd jolted all the breath out of me. I couldn't have whispered, let alone scream. He also managed to shake the magnifying glass out of my pocket. I heard it land on the ground, and a crunching, tinkling sound as he trod on it with a great big foot.

My brain hadn't stopped working, though, even if my voice had. A lot more was beginning to fall into place.

I'd obviously stumbled across an important meeting in the PTA hut. I'd seen Ron handing Mr Clyde a key. It *must* have been the key to the padlock on the stationery cupboard.

That meant Ron must have hidden the loot in there, and then gone out through the Hammett Avenue gate, almost certainly with Bernie. Mr Clyde must have escaped in the second getaway car, the one in Chandler Street that Inspector Raven had mentioned. The meeting in the hut was something they'd planned. Mr Clyde was probably going to get the money out of the stationery cupboard later, after school was over and everyone had gone home.

There were a few things I didn't understand, though. For instance, I didn't have a clear picture of what had gone on inside the school in those few minutes after the robbers had bumped into Miss Christie. She'd lost a shoe, so she'd probably put up a struggle. But they'd still managed to hide the money and get away very fast. Too fast, perhaps . . . they'd left a mask behind as a clue, hadn't they? And where *was* Miss Christie? Being held somewhere by the fourth robber, I supposed.

I had a nagging feeling that something wasn't right in all this. Something didn't quite fit.

I hardly had time to notice that we were in Hammett Avenue itself before I was bundled into a large red car. I ended up sitting in the middle of the back seat, with Ron and Bernie on either side of me. Mr Clyde got in the front and sat behind the steering wheel. He turned on the engine, but we didn't go anywhere.

Someone else was in the car too, in the front passenger seat. A figure wearing a hat, a raincoat with the collar pulled up, and a big pair of dark glasses. The Shadow!

My mum's always warning me about not getting into cars with strangers. Now I knew what she meant. I made a mental note never to get into this sort of situation again. Ever. But first I had to think of a way of getting out of the mess I was in, and fast. For once in my life, though, I didn't have any ideas.

'Well?' said the figure at last. The

Someone else was in the car too, in the front passenger seat.

voice was a surprise. It reminded me of someone, although I couldn't think who it was.

'The kid's been snooping around, boss,' said Mr Clyde. 'We didn't know what to do with her.'

They kept talking, but I didn't listen any more. I had to do something ... and if I couldn't escape, there was only one thing I *could* do.

Before anyone could stop me, I reached forward and grabbed at The Shadow's hat and dark glasses. There was a brief struggle, but I managed to knock them both off.

'You shouldn't have done that,' said The Shadow, turning to look at me. I was expecting to see a man's face, the face of an international criminal mastermind. But then I realized I was going to be wrong for the third time that day. I was staring at a face I knew.

The face of ... Miss Christie!

Chapter Nine

Ron and Bernie grabbed me and
pulled me back, but I wasn't interested in them. My mind was too busy
working overtime trying to understand what it all meant.

'I thought they'd kidnapped you!' I
blurted out.

Miss Christie threw back her head
and laughed. The sound chilled my
blood. It wasn't the sort of laugh
you'd expect from a teacher. Not even
a teacher as strict as Miss Christie.

'Kidnapped by these cretins?' she
said. 'They couldn't kidnap a baby
from a pram. If it wasn't for The
Shadow they'd be nothing, absolutely

nothing. Isn't that right, boys?'

'Yes, Boss,' the three men said together. They sounded like a class going through their times tables. 'We'd be nothing without you.'

'So, Sam,' said Miss Christie. 'You thought I was only your boring old teacher. You thought I spent all my time dreaming up difficult questions for surprise maths tests. But secretly I was devising a perfect bank robbery. And if it hadn't been for these dunderheads and one small problem, everything would have worked brilliantly.'

My mind was slowing down now. It was all beginning to make sense. The most important piece in the jigsaw puzzle had just fallen into place. Miss Christie had been the fourth robber, which was why everything had gone so smoothly when they'd got to the school.

'The whole thing's a set-up,' I said. 'You got a job at our school just so you could use it as a hiding place when you did the robbery. That's why you were so interested in the stationery cupboard from the start . . . No one would ever suspect one of the teachers was the leader of the gang. And you wouldn't have to worry about the money until the heat died down.'

'Well done, Samantha,' said Miss Christie with a nasty smile. 'Go to the top of the class. You're obviously not as stupid as your marks in my maths tests made me think.'

'So what went wrong?' I said. 'Was it losing one of your shoes?'

'Ah, so it was you who found it, was it?' said Miss Christie. 'Very clever of you. I was disguised like the others for the robbery, of course. I had my school clothes in a bag ready to change into when we got here. The mistake I made was allowing Ron to carry it. He left it open and must have dropped the shoe. I found out when it was too late to do anything about it. But by then it didn't matter.'

That answered another question for

me. If Ron was that careless with The Shadow's shoes, he was probably the one who had dropped his mask near the Hammett Avenue gate.

'It wasn't my fault, Boss,' he whined. 'It said in my horoscope . . .'

'Shut up about your blasted horoscope, imbecile!' snapped Miss Christie. She gave him a glare, the one she saved for children who got easy sums wrong, or who were late for school. I'd seen it before. Ron obviously had too. He shrank back and shut up.

'No, that wasn't the real problem,' she continued. A look of pain passed across her face. 'It was Class Nine . . . or at least, the tummy bug I caught from one of you. I started to feel ill at the bank, and when we got to the school I almost collapsed.'

Richard didn't know it, but he'd been right. I just hoped I'd be able to tell him some day.

'The plan had been for me to come in with Ron and Bernie and hide the money, then change into my school clothes and wait. I was going to say that I'd just arrived, and hadn't seen anything. But I felt so ill, I knew I'd never be able to pull it off. I decided to get him . . .' she nodded at Mr Clyde, '. . . to stand in for me. I left with Ron and Bernie in this car.

'I knew it was a gamble, but I thought we could fool old Pinkerton. All I needed was some time.'

The picture was clear in my mind, now. Mr Clyde going off in one direction; the other three coming into the school to hide the money, with Miss Christie looking ill and Ron scattering clues everywhere. They'd obviously met up somewhere outside the school to arrange for Mr Clyde to come back and pretend to be a teacher. But why had Ron and Bernie returned with the key so soon?

'I still think we ought to get the money and make a run for it now,' said Mr Clyde.

'You might be right,' said Miss

Christie scowling. 'Especially if young Samantha here has been telling all her friends what she knows.'

So that was it. So many things had gone wrong that they were getting a bit panicky. Correction. They were seriously rattled, and I was their biggest worry. I needed time too, time for someone to notice I wasn't in school, time for them to come looking for me.

Suddenly I had a terrific idea. It was a long shot, but I thought it might work.

'Well, Samantha?' Miss Christie was saying.

'OK, Miss, you win,' I said. 'But you're not going to like what you hear.'

'Try me,' she said. I paused for a second, just to drag it out a little longer.

'You're not the only one who can mastermind a set-up,' I said. 'I worked out a lot of it, and I told Inspector Raven everything. We knew that Mr

Clyde was a phony, and that Ron and Bernie were in the PTA hut. I went down there just so that they'd grab me ... and lead Inspector Raven to *you*. I was followed all the way. There must be hundreds of policemen out there just waiting to pounce.'

I was impressed. My story was so convincing I almost believed it myself. Ron fell for it hook, line and sinker, of course.

'Let's get out of here!' he yelled.

'Not so fast,' said Miss Christie. She looked through the windscreen. 'I don't see anyone who looks much like a policeman. I think she's bluffing.'

We all looked around. It was true. There were no police helicopters clattering in the sky, or police helmets sticking up on the roofs of the houses in Hammett Avenue. There was an old lady walking down the street towards us, but she didn't look much like a policeman, or like she'd be able to tackle a gang of hardened criminals.

'I wouldn't be so sure,' I said. I tried

to sound very confident, even though I wasn't. 'All I have to do is give the signal, and the street will be swarming with uniforms.'

Miss Christie threw her head back and produced another of those blood-curdling laughs.

'Go ahead then, Samantha,' she said. 'Give the signal, and let's see what happens!'

I gulped. It was now or never.

'OK,' I said, and jumped forward again between the two front seats. I slammed my hand down on the car horn as hard as I could. Ron and Bernie grabbed me, but not before I had the chance to sock Mr Clyde in the eye with an elbow, the one I use sometimes on Steven Greenstreet in the playground. Mr Clyde reacted in the same way Steven does, too.

'Oww!' he yelled, and clutched his eye. I wasn't going to go down without a fight, and I started kicking and punching anything within reach. In fact, I was keeping myself so busy

It was now or never....

that at first I didn't notice what happened next.

There was a sudden sound of wailing police sirens, and a police car with lights flashing screeched to a halt just in front of us. Mr Clyde tried to get away. The car roared, but I grabbed the steering wheel and we hit a lamp-post. We weren't going very fast, so it wasn't a bad crash – just enough to stop us.

Everything seemed to happen at once after that. I'd fallen head downwards between the two front seats, so I couldn't see what was going on. I did hear doors opening, feet pounding and lots of shouting, though. I managed to sit up and eventually I got out of the car. All the doors were open, and it was empty.

But Hammett Avenue wasn't empty anymore. It was full of policemen and police cars, and there was a police helicopter above it. It was as if a fairy godmother had heard what I'd said in the car and made it all come true with one wave of a magic wand.

'Well, well,' said a voice behind me. It certainly wasn't the voice of my fairy godmother. I turned round and saw Inspector Raven smiling down at me. 'So we meet again, young lady.'

He asked me if I was all right. I said I was.

'We've got them, Sir!' someone called out.

'Well done, lads!' said Inspector Raven.

I looked down the street, and saw Ron, Bernie and Mr Clyde being handcuffed and put into a police van.

But Miss Christie was nowhere to be seen.

The Shadow had escaped!

Chapter Ten

When Inspector Raven realized that The Shadow had vanished, he was absolutely furious. He ordered a search of the entire area around the school. But from the look on his face, I could tell he didn't think there was much hope.

I'd told him The Shadow was Miss Christie, and at first he wouldn't believe it. Like most men, he didn't think a woman could be a genius, so he'd always thought of The Shadow as a man. But then he realized how everything fitted together, and he knew I was right.

'That's probably the most important piece of information we've ever had about The Shadow,' he said. 'Not that it will do us much good at the moment. I'll bet she's long gone, by now . . . and what I'd like to know, Dixon, is how it happened. We almost had her, but you let her slip.'

'I'm sorry, Sir,' said Constable Dixon. 'I saw The Shadow get out of the car and make a run for it. I gave chase, but I'm afraid I tripped over my, er . . . dress. By the time I'd picked myself up, she'd gone. It was really weird, Sir. One minute she was there, and the next . . . well, she'd just completely disappeared.'

Now if you're wondering what Constable Dixon was doing in a dress, perhaps I should explain that he was in disguise himself. You remember that old lady I mentioned, the one walking up Hammett Avenue who didn't look like a policeman or as if she could tackle a gang of hardened criminals? Well, it had been Constable Dixon all along.

He looked pretty amazing, too. He was wearing a lady's green coat, and a long flowery dress underneath it. Both were covered in mud. He had some make-up on, but it was smudged, and his wig must have come off when he'd fallen over. I wasn't surprised that he'd tripped up, either. He was wearing big, black police boots. Just the sort of thing old ladies wear all the time, of course.

'Well, I want a full report on my desk by the end of the day, Dixon, and make sure there are no spelling mistakes,' said Inspector Raven. Then he turned to look at me. 'I'll be in the headmaster's office for the next hour or so. I've got a few questions to ask this young lady. If there's any news of The Shadow, bring it to me at once.'

'Yes, Sir,' said Constable Dixon, saluting. 'And by the way, Sir, we found this key on one of the robbers.' He held out the padlock key to the Inspector, who didn't say anything. He just took me by the arm and marched me back into school.

We went straight to Mr Pinkerton's office, where I told the headmaster and the Inspector the whole story from A to Z. I didn't have a lot of choice. Old Pinkerton nearly passed out several times, and the hairy caterpillars on his forehead spent most of their time hugging each other. But they went absolutely berserk when he found out about Miss Christie.

Inspector Raven didn't say much, except when I told him where I thought the key might fit.

'Are you sure?' he said.

'Positive,' I replied.

He picked up the phone, barked some instructions into it, and within a couple of minutes a constable was knocking at the door. The inspector gave him the key, and five minutes later there was a large sack on the carpet in front of us.

A sack full of money. Money stolen from the First National Savings Bank in Marple Street. We sat staring at it for a long moment in silence.

'Well,' said Mr Pinkerton. The two hairy caterpillars on his forehead were having a cuddle again. 'If it hadn't been for Robert, then I dread to think what might have happened. It's too awful to contemplate.'

He meant Richard, of course. It turned out he had run straight off to see Mr Pinkerton when I'd gone down to the PTA hut. He'd been too worried to keep quiet any more, so I owed him a big favour.

'Not that I believed him at first, though,' Mr Pinkerton was saying. 'I mean, it was such an incredible story . . . teachers being kidnapped, teachers who were really robbers. Mind you, I knew there was something odd about that Mr Clark from the moment I met him . . . But it was only when Stuart told me he'd seen you being carried out of the school by a strange man that I thought the time had come to do something.'

He meant Steven Greenstreet,

worse luck. Steven and The Feeble Five had been the boys who made all that noise going into the toilets next to the PTA hut. I should have guessed, really. They'd been sent to clean themselves up and get rid of the awful smell. Strange how things work out. If I'd never fooled them into rooting through the dustbins, they'd never have played a part in saving me.

They'd just been coming out of the toilets when they'd seen Ron, Bernie and Mr Clyde running out of the hut. They're so stupid they'd usually have trouble noticing a piano falling out of the sky and landing on their heads. But today they managed to notice that Ron and Bernie were strangers, and that Bernie just happened to have one of their classmates under his arm. They had ducked back before they'd been seen, waited a while, then run to Mr Pinkerton's office.

'I phoned the police,' said Mr Pinkerton, 'and it was very lucky for you that Inspector Raven had only just left the school.'

'I was still in the car when they called me from the station,' said the Inspector, 'and we set up the operation immediately. I knew there was something fishy going on, so I already had our special team ready and waiting. Then we spotted the car with you in it, and moved in . . .'

It was all pretty impressive, really. Or it would have been if they'd managed to catch The Shadow. But I didn't say anything. I had a feeling I was in enough trouble as it was.

'. . . That only leaves one loose end to be tied up, I think – doesn't it, young lady?' the Inspector was saying.

'Sorry?' I said. 'I'm not sure what you're getting at.'

'It's very simple, Samantha,' said the Inspector. 'What are we going to do with *you*? Let me see . . . withholding evidence, interfering with police business, failing to report a serious crime . . . If you were a few years older, you'd be looking at some

pretty serious charges. They could
get a grown-up at least three years
wearing pyjamas with arrows on
them. You played a pretty dangerous
game, too. What have you got to say
for yourself?'

It looked like I was in another tight
spot. That's typical of grown-ups.
You do them a small favour, like solve
a major case and give them the best

lead they've ever had on an international criminal mastermind, and
they're still not satisfied. I'd learned a
lot today, but there was one thing I'd
known all along, and it hadn't changed
much. It's tough being a kid.

'I didn't *mean* to do anything
wrong,' I said. 'I would have told you,
but I didn't think you'd believe me
without any proof. I thought you'd
probably tell me to run along like a
good little girl.'

The Inspector smiled.

'Maybe I would have done,' he said.
'And maybe I wouldn't. That's for me
to know, and you to find out . . . But I
think we'll give you the benefit of the
doubt. Just remember, though – you
were lucky. It could all have been a lot
worse.'

The headmaster was nodding in the
background, and the hairy caterpillars
were doing exercises on his forehead.
I could tell he just wanted everything
to work out right in a big happy
ending, the sort where you could say

... 'and they all lived happily ever after.' Especially the headmaster.

'Does that mean I'm off the hook?' I said.

'I suppose it does, Sam,' said the Inspector.

'Thanks,' I said. 'Can I go now?'

They said I could, although the Inspector said he'd need to get a statement from me in a day or two. I was an important witness, so the case wasn't over for me just yet.

I went to the door and opened it.

'Next time I'll tell you what's happening a little sooner,' I said. 'That's a promise.'

'Let's just hope for your sake there won't be a next time,' said the Inspector. I knew he was giving me a warning, but it didn't worry me all that much. I had a bigger problem to face, one that brought me out in a cold sweat just thinking about it.

I wasn't all that worried about Richard's dad's magnifying glass, although it was going to take me a long time to save up enough money to pay for it. No, it was worse than that. I had to go home and face my mum and dad. I'd have to tell them the story, and I could just see their faces, especially when they heard the part about me being involved with the police. I had a feeling I'd be seeing Dad's Stern Father act again pretty soon.

But that's OK. It's all in a day's work for Sam Marlowe, world-famous girl detective.

'Here's looking at you, Sir,' I said to the Inspector.

I pulled the brim of my imaginary detective hat down over one eye, shut the door behind me and walked down the corridor back to class.

Who knows? In a day or two I might even have another case to solve . . .